MR. MEN
LITTLE MISS
ANIMAL WORLD

Roger Hargreaves

Original concept by
Roger Hargreaves

Written and illustrated by
Adam Hargreaves

"The answer is hibernation," replied Little Miss Tiny. "Some squirrels find a nice snug, cosy hollow in a tree and go to sleep through the coldest part of the winter."

"Thank you, Little Miss Tiny. Now we know how squirrels keep warm, but I wonder, how do penguins keep warm in freezing Antarctica? Let's go there now and see who our reporter is," said Little Miss Curious.

It was Little Miss Hug.

Little Miss Hug was filming the penguins all huddled together.

"Hello, Little Miss Curious," she said. "This is how penguins keep warm. They all huddle together in a group. It's like a big group hug!"

"Penguins also have very tightly-packed feathers to insulate them. Mr Snow, on the other hand, doesn't need anything to keep him warm. In fact, he's here on his summer holiday!"

"Now, walruses don't have feathers, but they have a very thick layer of fat to keep them warm," continued Little Miss Hug. "That layer of fat is called blubber. Walruses can happily swim in the freezing sea."

"Just looking at Mr Snow makes me feel cold!" exclaimed Little Miss Curious. "Thank you, Little Miss Hug."

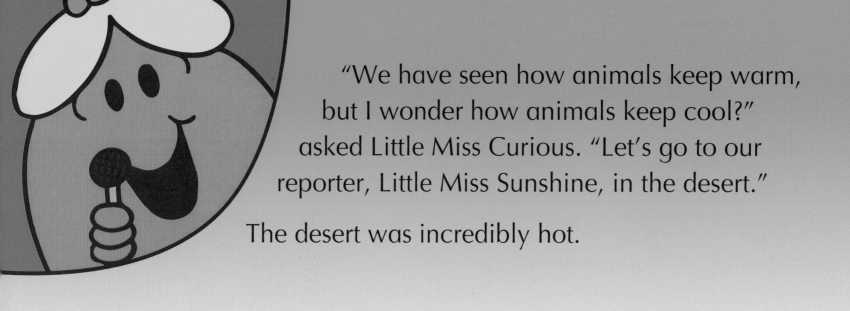

"We have seen how animals keep warm, but I wonder how animals keep cool?" asked Little Miss Curious. "Let's go to our reporter, Little Miss Sunshine, in the desert."

The desert was incredibly hot.

"Hello, Little Miss Curious. Animals in the desert live underground where it is cooler and lots of them only come out at night when the sun has gone down," said Little Miss Sunshine.

"Other animals, like lizards, look for shade.
Very few stay out in the midday sun.
Would you like a glass of water,
Little Miss Stubborn?"

"Desert animals have also adapted to the very dry conditions by needing very little water to drink," said Little Miss Curious.

"That's right," agreed Little Miss Sunshine. "But the desert hare has another way of keeping cool. It has enormous ears which help it to lose heat and cool down!"

"Now, there's a good question," said Little Miss Curious.
"Which animal has the biggest ears?"

"That's easy," said Little Miss Sunshine, and showed her
the elephants.

Who did indeed have the biggest ears.
And the longest noses.
Even longer than Mr Nosey's nose.

"I don't think Mr Nosey can do that with his nose!" laughed
Little Miss Curious, as the elephant sprayed him with water.

As the camera panned round, Little Miss Curious noticed someone hiding.

It was Little Miss Shy.
What was Little Miss Shy doing?
Was she hiding because she was so shy?

No, not this time. She was in a hide from where she could watch the animals without scaring them off. Not that you can imagine Little Miss Shy scaring anything!

"What are you watching?" asked Little Miss Curious.

"That crocodile," whispered Little Miss Shy into her microphone, blushing.

Little Miss Curious looked at the river, but she couldn't see anything.

It was a very well-hidden crocodile.

"Can you see it?" Little Miss Curious asked her audience.

"I wonder how other animals hide?" asked Little Miss Curious. "Here in the wood I have found a hedgehog which was so well camouflaged I nearly missed it. Mind those prickles, Little Miss Tiny!"

"Let's go and ask Mr Impossible in the rainforest."

"The python has markings that make it blend into the dappled sunlight of the forest," said Mr Impossible.

The python was as long as Mr Tickle's arm. And just as wriggly!

"Whereas the stick insect uses its body shape to disguise itself as a … well, a stick!" laughed Mr Impossible.

But the best camouflage was that of the chameleon.

"It can change colour to look exactly the same as its background," explained Mr Impossible. "Just like me!"

And Mr Impossible changed colour and disappeared!

"Bye, Mr Impossible," laughed Little Miss Curious. "Look, there is Little Miss Splendid. Now, she wants to stand out, just like that bird of paradise."

"Back here in our little wood, Little Miss Tiny has found a hopping rabbit," said Little Miss Curious.

"Can you think of any other animals that hop?"

"That's right!"

"Kangaroos! And here's Mr Bounce with one down under in Australia."

"G'day, Little Miss Curious!" said Mr Bounce.

"You're upside down!" exclaimed Little Miss Curious.
"Is that because you're down under?"

"No!" cried Mr Bounce. "It's because Mr Muddle is holding
the camera upside down!"

"Isn't it amazing how each animal on the planet has evolved differently?" said Little Miss Curious.

"Cheetahs are incredibly fast."

"Tortoises are very slow."

"Sharks are really scary."

"Giraffes are very tall."

"And mice are very small and very quiet."

"What is the loudest animal on the planet?" asked Little Miss Tiny.

Little Miss Tiny guessed a roaring lion and Little Miss Curious thought it might be a trumpeting elephant.

But Mr Noisy had an altogether more surprising answer.

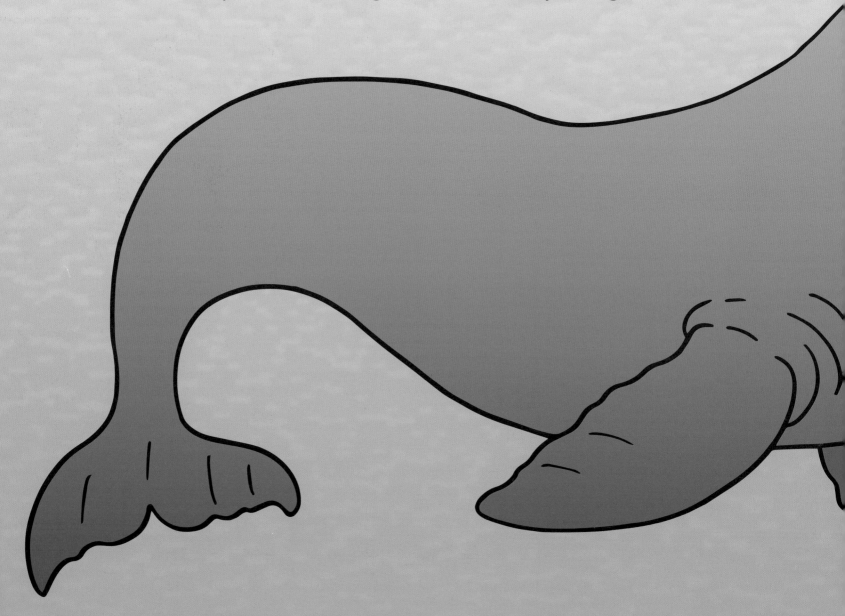

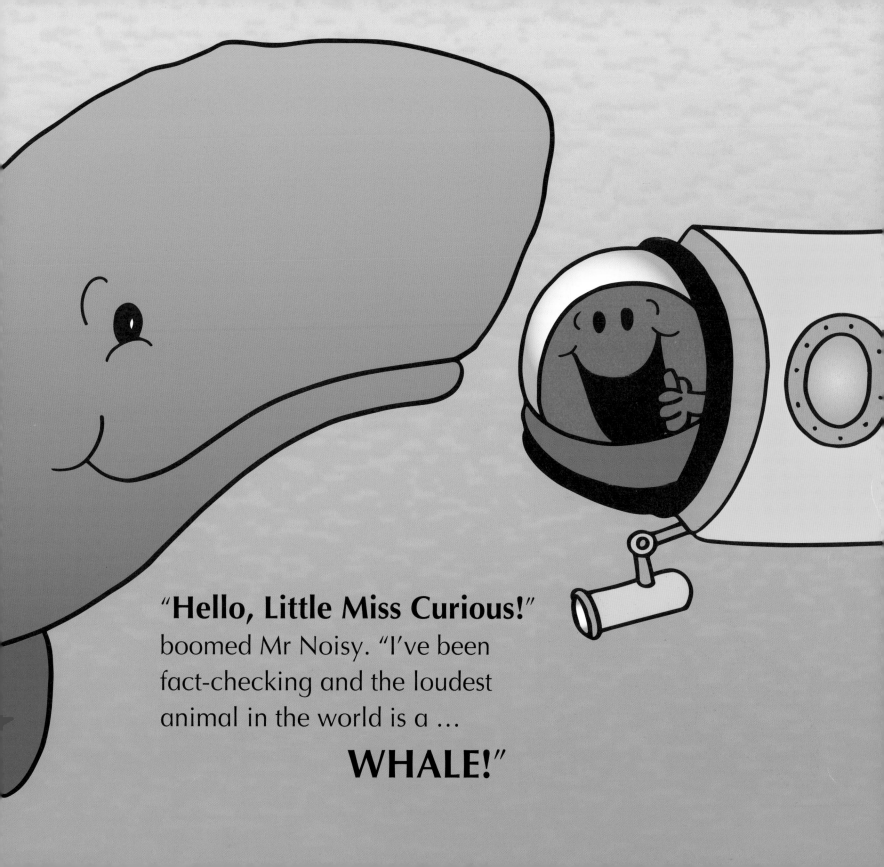

"**Hello, Little Miss Curious!**" boomed Mr Noisy. "I've been fact-checking and the loudest animal in the world is a ...

WHALE!"

"Blimey! I now also know that Mr Noisy is the loudest person in the world! Let's go to Mr Funny and see what funny animals he has to show us."

"Hello, everyone! I have a tapir here," chuckled Mr Funny. "Just look at his nose!"

Mr Funny then showed all the other funny animals he had found.

There was the potoo bird.

And the platypus, an animal with fur, a duck's beak and webbed feet.

And the blue-tongued skink.

"Ostriches are funny looking birds," added Mr Funny. "And they are so big that they can't fly. A bird that can't fly, how silly is that?"

"That is silly," replied Little Miss Curious. "Talking of silly things, here's Mr Silly in Nonsenseland."

"Here in Nonsenseland," said Mr Silly, "we have birds that fly backwards ...

... into trees!"

"And cows that wear wellington boots."

"And chickens that lay Easter eggs."

"And my favourite of all, worms who sleep in hammocks!"

"Now, it's goodbye from me and the friendly woodland animals," said Little Miss Curious. "We have just one more animal to show you. So it's over to Mr Lazy in the jungle with a sleepy sloth."

"Hello, Mr Lazy."

"Hello ... ?"

But there was no reply from
Mr Lazy, for he, and the sloth,
were in a very deep sleep!